My Brother Is Afraid of Just About Everything

Lois Osborn
Pictures by Jennie Williams

Albert Whitman & Company, Niles, Illinois

Library of Congress Cataloging in Publication Data

Osborn, Lois.
  My brother is afraid of just about everything.

  (Concept book. Level 2)
  Summary: The narrator can't understand his little
brother's many fears until a large, panting dog
happens by.
  [1. Fear—Fiction. 2. Brothers and sisters—
Fiction] I. Williams, Jennie, 1949– , ill.
II. Title. III. Series.
PZ7.Q797My   [E]   81-23981
ISBN 0-8075-5324-7 (lib. bdg.)   AACR2

Dedicated to the memory of
Emily Catlett

My little brother is afraid of just about everything.

Whenever there's a thunderstorm,
I know where to find him.
Underneath the bed.

So I take him out first.
Then I empty the tub.

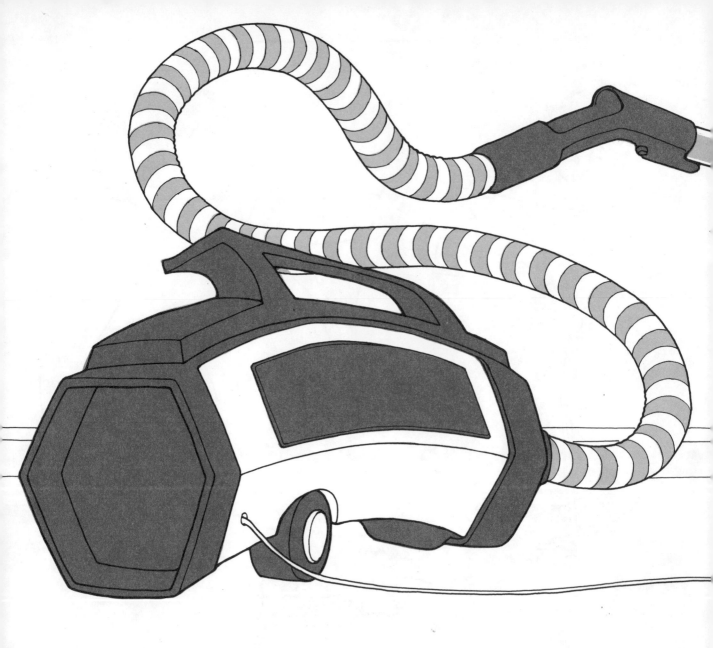

Yesterday my mother started to vacuum.
My brother started to howl.

Maybe he thinks the vacuum cleaner is
a monster. He sure acts that way.
So my mother asked me to take him for a walk.

We went past my school. "See?"
I said. "That's where you'll be
going in a couple of years."

I could tell by my brother's face
what he thought about *that*.

We met some of my friends at the
playground. They think my brother
is cute. "What's your name?" and
"How old are you?" they asked.

Did my brother answer them?
No-o-o, of course not.

He just buried his face
in my stomach,
the way he always does.

On our way home, we came to some
railroad tracks. A train was coming,
so we waited to cross.

Most kids think trains are pretty exciting.
They wave at the engineer.
They count cars.
But not my brother.

His arms went around me like boa constrictors.
I couldn't have shaken him loose
if I'd wanted to.

Back home, we sat together under the
big tree in our backyard.
I decided it was time we had a talk.

"Look," I said to him, "did thunder
and lightning ever hurt you?"
He shook his head.

"Or the mailman, or the vacuum cleaner?"
He shook his head again.

"Then how come you're so scared
of everything?" I asked.

My brother's face drooped. The corners
of his mouth turned down and quivered.
His shoulders came up to his ears.
His big eyes looked at me.

I felt like patting him on the back
and saying that everything was okay.

But instead I said, "Look,
you've got to get tough.
It's stupid to keep on being afraid
of things that won't hurt you."

Then I saw a great big, happy smile
spread across my brother's face.
He was looking at something behind me.
I didn't even have to ask what it was.

Nothing else could make my brother
look that happy.
It had to be—a dog!

I tried.
I tried very hard.

I shut my eyes and pretended
the dog wasn't there.

I took deep breaths so my heart
wouldn't beat so fast.

I clenched my hands so they
would stop trembling.

I prayed the dog would go away.

Then I felt its feet upon my shoulders.
I thought of sharp claws.

I felt its rough, wet tongue against
the back of my neck.
I thought of all those teeth.

That did it!

I couldn't get into the house fast enough!
Across the yard I ran.
I yanked open the screen door and
quickly slammed it shut.
I even hooked it.

Safe behind the door, I stood,
catching my breath.

Then I went to the window.
I knew what I would see.

Yes, there was my brother,
with his arms around that dog.

I watched them play together.
I watched them for a long time.

I suppose that dog would have
played with me, too, if I
had been outside.

But I stayed inside.

I felt bad about it,
but I stayed inside.

Oh well, everybody's afraid of
something, I guess . . .

LOIS OSBORN wrote and illustrated her first picture book when she was nine years old. The book was never published, but it sparked a lifelong habit of writing stories and poems for fun.

Mrs. Osborn taught elementary school for many years. She has four grown children—two sons and two daughters—and ten grandchildren. *My Brother Is Afraid of Just About Everything* is her first published book.

JENNIE WILLIAMS studied art at Parsons School of Design in New York City and St. Martins School of Art in London. She began her illustrating career in London. Somehow she managed to do the illustrations for *My Brother Is Afraid of Just About Everything* while taking care of her six- month-old son and helping her husband, a film producer, remodel their old New England house.